THE HAUNTING OF
APARTMENT 101

Darby Creek
A division of Lerner Publishing Group, Inc.
241 First Avenue North
Minneapolis, MN 55401 U.S.A.

Website address: www.lernerbooks.com

Cover and interior photographs © Victor Pelaez
Torres/Dreamstime.com (building); © iStockphoto
.com/appletat (silhouette).

Main body text set in Janson Text LT Std 12/17.5.
Typeface provided by Adobe Systems.

Library of Congress
Cataloging-in-Publication Data
Atwood, Megan.
    The haunting of apartment 101 / by Megan
Atwood.
       p.   cm. — (The paranormalists ; case #01)
    Summary: When popular, pretty classmate
asks best friends Jinx and Jackson, high school
sophomores, to investigate a haunting at her
father's apartment, Jackson is sympathetic and
convinces Jinx to trust him, despite her skepticism
about Emily's true intentions.
    ISBN 978–0–7613–8332–1 (lib. bdg. : alk.
paper)
    [1. Haunted places—Fiction. 2. Apartment
houses—Fiction. 3. Supernatural—Fiction.
4. Best friends—Fiction. 5. Friendship—Fiction.]
I. Title.
PZ7.A8952Hau 2012
[Fic]—dc23   2011046442

Manufactured in the United States of America
1 – PP –7/15/12

THE PARANORMALISTS
CASE 1

THE HAUNTING OF
APARTMENT 101

MEGAN ATWOOD

darbycreek

MINNEAPOLIS

THE PARANORMALISTS

Paranormalists Blog—
WE HAVE LIFTOFF!

Hello, Paranormalists fans (and my mom)! So here's our site's first blog post. I know, I know, it's been a long time coming—almost three months since the launch of the site—but I wanted to get everything in order. And the investigation team had some business to attend to—namely, investigating paranormal phenomena in this great city of Portland, OR. We're your local ghost-banshee-psychic hunters. And we're real good, even if we are only in high school.

With that, I'd like to give a shout-out to NO ONE AT MY SCHOOL. You all suck. Love, Jinx.

Anyway, I digress. Here's a recap of our findings so far. I'm not going to lie, they were a little disappointing.

HAWTHORNE DISTRICT

We had a tip-off that a warehouse in the Hawthorne district was haunted. I had JUST gotten my EVP and my EMF monitors (EVP = electronic voice phenomena—soooo cool! It can detect voices on different frequencies. And EMF means electromagnetic field. Like, if there's lotsa energy radiating from a place. Mine has a temp gauge too, so I can tell when the ghosties come near. Please don't faint from the coolness.)

Anyway, the investigation team went and checked it out. I could only stay out to midnight (lame!), but that was enough to know that the warehouse WAS haunted. By skaters who partied there. The only EMFs I found were the ones generated from being yelled at.

EVP: Nada

EMF: See above

Video: Doesn't matter. Though we could have busted a bunch of underage drinkers.

Temperature: You know, hot. It was freaking July.

Verdict: So not haunted, it hurt.

Before the next outing—**BARBUR TRANSIT CENTER**—I overheard some bus drivers talking about how sometimes the buses started up on their own overnight. How cool is that? This time we needed an overnight. And because I have the strictest parents in the world, I couldn't do it. (I need to figure out something.) Investigator 2 took the lead on this (even though we decided he'd be the "get rid of the ghosts" guy) and stayed overnight with my babies (I mean, equipment). And guess what? Not one bus started up.

People lie. Ghosts don't. This is why I like the dead.

EVP: Jackson (I mean, Investigator 2) snoring

EMF: Blerg

Video: Bus drivers drinking coffee

Temperature: Guess

Verdict: Really not haunted

Disappointing, no? For a city that's supposed to be pretty full of paranormal activity, I'm bummed. Paranormalist fans, help us find the haunted here!! I KNOW they're out there.

But for now, keep believing, keep seeing, and keep checking back while I tweak the site. And remember, the Paranormalists "SEEK THE TRUTH AND FIND THE CAUSE!!" (What do you think of our new tagline? Cool, huh?)

—Investigator 1 (Jinx)

CHAPTER 1

"No, no, no, no, no!" Jinx tapped hard on her laptop, almost breaking the delete key. She looked around the room to make sure no one had suddenly materialized in her room.

Still alone. Just as she liked it.

She'd been working on her site for over an hour and still she couldn't get the graphics just right. The site was everything. It had to look great.

She got up from her black plastic *Ikea* chair and did a lap around her room. She touched the

Pixies poster for good luck, took another lap, and ran her hand through her short, bleach-blonde-and-pink hair. And then . . . she had it.

Jinx let out a whoop that scared her cat, Poindexter, who had just meandered intothe room. She mumbled an apology and sat back down at her computer, tap-tapping away, knees bouncing.

She sat back and stared in admiration at her handiwork. She was good. Real good.

Grabbing her iPhone, she flopped on her bed and rang Jackson. After four rings, he picked up. She could just picture him in his superclean room, picking up his ancient flip cell. The boy was seriously outdated. Lucky for him, he had Jinx. Well, her and the rest of the school. Because *he* was popular.

"Jackson!" Jinx gasped into the phone.

"Jinx!" Jackson mocked back.

"No time for your mockery. You must look at the site."

Jackson went quiet, and Jinx started to hear tapping in the background. "Sooo . . . what am I looking at?" Jackson said.

"Duh. The ghost I put on the front page."

"Yeah . . . I don't see a ghost."

Jinx jumped off her bed and stared at her screen. "Oh, I didn't press Enter. OK, refresh and see what you see."

"And when I see this awesome ghost on the site, should I prepare to see the new addition where you tell people we're charging them?"

Jinx flopped back on her bed. "Jackson, we've been through this. I hate people. Therefore, from now on, we charge."

"You don't hate people."

"I do. All of them. Except you and my parents and my snot-head brother—don't tell him that. Have you refreshed the site yet?"

"Yeah . . . here we go." A pause, then Jackson said, "This is awesome, Jinx! Seriously spooky!"

Jinx smiled huge to herself. She'd never admit it, but she always wanted Jackson's approval. Always.

"Sweet. I'm going to work on the audio tonight. Pretty soon, we'll be getting megahits. And it's about time. I've been working on this site for how long?"

Jackson was quiet for a minute. "Almost a year? Since beginning of freshman year. You know, around the time you decided that high school was going to suck and that you wanted to freak out our entire class. And bleach your hair and start wearing black and start being mean . . ."

Jinx rolled her eyes. "Whatevs. High schoolers are the worst people on Earth. They deserve it. Besides, my hair looks awesome."

"You know we're both *in* high school, right?"

Jinx said breezily, "Yes, but it's temporary, like syphilis. And our website is freaking penicillin. Are you coming over tonight for *Ghost Hunters?*"

"Don't I always?"

Jinx could hear the smile in his voice. She smiled too. "Bring the Twizzlers," she said and hung up.

CHAPTER 2

J ackson hung up the phone and grinned.

That was Jinx all right: abrupt, prickly (even before her transformation), and, though he'd never say this to her face, soft on the inside.

In middle school, no one knew who she was. Jackson remembered the hurt looks on her face when people forgot her name. A name that, admittedly, was incredibly plain. In fact, it even rhymed with plain—Jane.

The summer before freshman year, Jinx had unleashed her tough side. She turned, well, weird. All of a sudden, everyone knew who she was. Kids at school even gave her the nickname, Jinx. She loved it. She had wanted to be anyone else besides plain Jane. And she got her wish.

It took Jackson a while to get used to the change, but once he saw that Jinx loved her new nickname, he started calling her that too. It made her happy, so why wouldn't he?

The website was what turned everything around. After eighth-grade graduation, after the fourth person simultaneously forgot Jane's name and invited Jackson to a party (skipping her), she turned to Jackson and said, "I'm starting a webwsite." In two weeks, the Paranormalists site was born, and so was the new Jane. And Jackson's secret wish got louder in his head.

Sure, in one year, they'd only gone ghost hunting a few times. And those outings did nothing to help Jackson believe. But surely things would pick up?

"Jackson!" His mom's shout interrupted his look back. "Help with dinner? I can never do the seasoning on the tacos right."

"Coming!" He flipped off his computer and trotted down the stairs. He turned the corner to the kitchen and saw his mom crumbling beef in the skillet. Jackson took the wooden spoon from her, effortlessly slipping into kitchen mode.

"Hey, are Grant and Hamilton coming back tonight?"

His mom shook her head. "Nope. Too much schoolwork." She looked at Jackson and winked. "Their type of schoolwork, I'm sure."

Jackson smiled. "Studying German, you mean? Like, I don't know . . . *Jägermeister*?"

His mom shuddered. "I hope when you start college drinking, you have the good sense to drink something less stupid-inducing. But then again, my straight-A boy will probably actually study." She reached to tousle his hair and he ducked.

"Someone's got to take care of you," he said and then immediately wished he hadn't. His mom was quiet for a second and then turned to him.

"Jackson, you know I can take care of myself, right? It's not your job. Even your dad didn't 'take care of me'—we were partners. I miss him every day . . . but we took care of each other. OK?"

Jackson stared at the beef and stirred like his life depended on it. Even four years after his dad's death, the wound still felt fresh.

He cleared his throat and tried to lighten the mood. "No worries, Mom. Anyway, I'm trying to talk Jinx into actually working with people through the website. You know, actual investigations. She wants to charge if we do that."

His mom rummaged through the refrigerator, her voice light and airy. "Oh, really? She thinks there's enough paranormal activity in Portland to get you some money?"

"Yep. And why not? I mean, who hasn't had something weird happen to them, right? Some chairs moving . . . lightbulbs flickering . . . strange telepathic moments . . . maybe things are happening all the time, right in front of us. It would be cool to find out for sure." He didn't add out loud his secret wish: *Like if Dad is watching us right now and trying to communicate.*

His mom smiled at him as if she could read his thoughts, but said, "Well, I hope you can find some cases."

He stirred the beef some more and added his own homemade taco seasoning. The smell in the kitchen bloomed and his stomach growled. "Yeah . . . but first I have to talk Jinx into, you know, trusting other people."

His mom set the table with two plates and silverware. She chuckled. "Oh, I don't think that will be too hard. She adores you, and let's face it—beneath everything, Jinx is soft on the inside."

Strange telepathic moments.

CHAPTER 3

Jocks. Cheerleaders. Dorks. Overachievers. Drama geeks. Forgettables.

Cattle. They were all cattle. The bell had just wrung and already Jinx felt tired. Sophomore year had come, and there she was on the first day of the year, standing in the same hallway, seeing the same people, thinking the same thoughts.

Someone bumped into her shoulder and said, "Watch out, freak!"

Jinx smiled. Freak. That was way better

than being a Forgettable. She turned around and said, "Bump into me again, and *you'd* better watch out." She said it quietly, but the guy turned to look at her—a jock, for sure—a hint of fear in his eyes.

Maybe school wouldn't be so bad. Having a reputation as someone who dabbled in the dark arts, whatever that meant, had its advantages. If they knew she was really a tech nerd, she wouldn't garner half as much respect.

Jackson sidled up to her. "Making friends already?"

She smiled. "He started it."

Jackson said, "That's Travis. He's actually a pretty nice guy. We play football together. I think he's dating Emily."

"Like I care." Yep, a jock. Jinx sighed and anger traveled up her back. How could Jackson be friends with these people? "And anyway, he's so nice, he called me a freak. Whatever. I wouldn't want to interrupt you two playing with your balls." She bumped her shoulder against his. "Now, to homeroom?"

"Homeroom."

They walked side by side, people calling "hey" to Jackson every two steps. Everyone ignored Jinx—but at least it was because they were afraid of her. She scowled at everyone who looked her in the eye. She knew that Jackson probably got a lot of crap for being friends with her, but she knew he would never dump her as a friend or talk trash behind her back. Another reason he was a cut above the cattle the high school raised.

It was two minutes before the bell was due to ring, and Jackson and Jinx were four doors down from homeroom when they ran into Emily.

Her face was paler than pale and her hair dirty blonde. She ran right into Jinx and Jackson and jumped back as if she'd been electrocuted.

Jinx said, "Watch it!" at the same time that Jackson said, "Emily, are you OK?"

Emily looked up with huge blue haunted eyes, looking like a startled woodland creature.

Anger twitched in Jinx again. In middle school, Emily had called Jinx "Roberta" and looked through her like she didn't exist. She had invited Jackson everywhere, though. Jinx's eyes narrowed. She couldn't say she was unhappy to see her looking like a mess.

Emily stammered, "So . . . sorry," and tried to move away from them. Jackson caught her arm.

"Emily, if something's wrong, you can tell us."

Jinx tapped her foot. "The bell is going to ring, dingus. Come on, we have to get to homeroom."

Emily looked back and forth between Jinx and Jackson. She shook her head. "It's nothing. And anyway . . . no one can help us."

With that, the bell rang and Emily took off down the hall.

CHAPTER 4

Jackson stared down the hall at Emily's retreating form. He could tell she'd lost weight. And she *never* left the house without makeup. Something was majorly wrong.

Jinx grabbed his arm. "Homeroom, now!" They ran to their door and managed to slink into two seats in the back while the teacher had his back turned.

The teacher turned around and said, "I'm Mr. Rallston. I'm new here, so that means you can get away with murder and I'll have no idea if it's against the rules. And I look forward to you all making me despise this year so much that I never teach again." He smiled a big smile.

The class sat silent, shocked.

"Just kidding! Well, I *am* new. But I love teaching and it'll take more than a few murder-getting-away-withs to make me quit."

Jackson glanced over at Jinx. Her face was rapt. She leaned forward, a smile playing on her lips. What, did she like this joker? Jackson looked at Mr. Rallston and tried to see him through a girl's eyes. He supposed he was good looking. If a person was into way-old types.

Not that he was jealous. He was just looking out for Jinx. Crushes on teachers led to bad places.

He turned his attention back to Mr. Rallston, but it wavered quickly. He thought about Emily again. He needed to talk to her. He'd have to do it when Jinx wasn't around— maybe during lunch period. He glanced at Jinx again and saw she was still staring with rapt attention at Mr. Rallston.

Evidently, she *was* into way-old types.

At lunch, Jackson scanned the crowd for Emily. He didn't know for sure if they had the same lunch period, but it was worth a try. His teammates from football called out to him to sit with them. He smiled and held up his finger. He kept looking and couldn't find Emily anywhere. Maybe she was in Jinx's period. Briefly, he wondered who Jinx sat with at lunch, but the thought slipped away. She could take care of herself. He set down his huge lunch: school cafeteria burger, fries, and cherry pie. And an apple. After all, he wasn't a total slob. He believed in eating healthy.

"What's up?" he said as he sat down.

The table high-fived all around. They'd been practicing for a good two weeks, since before school started, so they'd seen a lot of one another.

"What do you think coach will do at practice today? Last week was killer, dude."

Jackson took a huge bite of his burger and nodded. He rotated his shoulder—on Saturday he'd barely been able to move it. Being quarterback meant more than being a team member, though. It meant being a leader. As a sophomore, he wasn't the starting QB yet, but he wanted to be. And as his mom said, "Behave how you want to be."

"We need it, though, if we're going to get to state this year," Jackson said. "Last year sucked big time when we blew that game."

The team nodded and then slipped into the inevitable who's-hot-this-year talk. Jackson spaced off and stared out the windows. He thought that kind of talk was pretty boring, though he often agreed with the conclusions. But still, sometimes Jinx had a point about his friends.

Just as he was smiling to himself, he noticed a skinny, stringy-haired girl pass by. Emily. He stood up fast and mumbled to the team, "See ya." Clearing his place, he threw the garbage away and stacked the tray on top of some others, keeping an eye on Emily the whole time. She slipped out of the lunchroom and Jackson followed.

She took the stairs to the second floor. Jackson called out, "Emily," so he wouldn't freak her out, but her form kept climbing. She disappeared into the hall.

Jackson reached the top of the stairs and looked for her. She was standing by her locker with her forehead resting on it. Jackson approached her like he would a wild animal.

"Emily?" As he got closer, he could see she was crying.

She turned to look at him. "Jackson, things are really bad right now." She sniffled and drew in a huge breath. She said so quietly Jackson could barely hear, "Maybe I could use your help."

Jackson got closer and put his hand on her shoulder briefly. "Anything."

She sniffled and leaned her back against the locker. "You're friends with that girl, Jinx, right? She maybe could help too."

Jackson couldn't help it. He wrinkled his nose and said, "Jinx?" No one ever wanted her help. "What for?"

Emily turned and faced him head on. "I'm being haunted."

CHAPTER 5

"I just don't know how many ways I can say no to this." Jinx took an angry bite from her Twizzler and chewed hard. Jackson had been poking at her for over an hour, ever since they'd left school for the day.

Jackson sighed. They sat in Jinx's basement looking over Jinx's equipment for the millionth time. Jinx never got tired of it.

Jackson pointed to one of the devices. "Think about this—when else would you get a chance to use this for something *real*? For an actual case that we didn't overhear or read about in the paper. This is a person asking for help, Jinx!"

Jinx finally put the device down and sat forward, using the Twizzler to point at Jackson to punctuate her words.

"OK, let's go over this again. One: Emily is a shallow buttwad. She always has been. She's probably jerking me around because that's what her kind does. I don't trust her as far as I can throw her, and you know how far that is." She flexed a tiny bicep. "And two: Why would I help someone who thought my name was Roberta? Who is named Roberta? Ever?" She sat back and finished her Twizzler with a snap, taking another one out of the package.

"Those are bad for you, you know. All that sugar."

Jinx snorted. "Let me guess what you had for lunch—burger and fries?"

"And an apple," Jackson said defensively.

"Whatever. The answer is still no."

Jackson sat back hard against the couch. He picked up the EVP device and fiddled with it. It took all Jinx's willpower to not tell him to set it down. After a minute, she gently took it away from him and put it on her lap. Where it belonged. She began to sense Jackson brooding next to her.

"Why do you want to help her so bad anyway?"

Jackson shrugged, but Jinx knew the answer. He was a nice guy. He knew what it felt like to have an insurmountable problem. She remembered the year his dad died. She was devastated—he was like a second father to her—but Jackson was inconsolable. For two months, Jinx would go over and just sit with him, neither of them saying a word. In fact, he didn't say a word to anyone during that time. She wasn't sure he'd get through it. Little by little, he started talking more often. She could almost feel the weight on him lessening slowly. It was still there, though, and she knew it came back with every hard case and sob story that came across his lap.

She twisted her lip and started pacing. It *would* be nice to investigate an actual case.

Even if she hated people, she loved the idea of meeting a ghost.

Out of the corner of her eye, she saw Jackson sit up a little straighter, a small smile playing on his lips. He knew her too well.

"Wipe that grin off your face. I haven't said yes yet."

Jackson nodded—a knowing nod—and didn't say a thing.

"OK, so this Emily said she was being haunted?" Jinx asked. Jackson nodded again. "Did she say where?"

"She didn't say a whole bunch about it. Just that she and her dad moved into a new apartment and it's haunted."

Jinx scoffed. "That's all you got from her?"

Jackson said, calmly, "I wanted to talk to you first."

Jinx clamped her mouth shut, pacing some more. On one of her trips around the room, she grabbed a Twizzler, the last one of the package. She left the empty cellophane there, and Jackson picked it up and threw the thing away.

"*If* we help her . . . and I mean a big *if* . . . we're charging her a fee."

Jackson sighed. "Jinx, do we really have to?"

Jinx stopped and glared at him. "It's a good model when you're forced to help people you hate."

Jackson sighed again and picked the EVP device back up. Jinx couldn't help it. "Put that down," she snapped.

Jackson let it go and put his hands up in surrender, a have-a-conniption-why-don't-you look on his face.

"We charge a $400 flat fee, $200 each," Jinx said. "And we *both* do an overnight—I'll figure out a way to get out of the house."

Jackson smiled a broad smile. "I knew you'd do it!"

Jinx shook her head. "You're not as smart as you think you are, you know." But she had to admit, he sort of was. Her heart raced as she thought about an actual case. Maybe, finally, she'd see a real haunting.

CHAPTER 6

"OK, just approach her slowly, no sudden moves. Just be honest and open, and you'll do fine." Jackson put his hand on Emily's shoulder and added, "Twizzlers wouldn't hurt."

Emily gave him a blank stare and then said, "It sounds like you're talking about a dog."

A rabid dog, Jackson thought to himself, but he forced a smile. "She's just . . . particular."

Emily nodded and Jackson saw her eyes fill with tears. "As long as you guys can make these . . . things go away. I haven't slept in three weeks! I can't eat. I can't concentrate. It's horrible!"

Jackson felt the familiar tug at his stomach that came when someone around him was hurting. He squared his shoulders. "We'll make this better. Jinx is brilliant at this stuff." He didn't add that they had yet to come across a real ghost. Or that if they needed to get rid of one, he'd have no idea how. Jinx had given him the job to research that stuff—but he'd come up with nothing. He figured it was just a detail to figure out later, and he hoped Jinx just trusted him to come through.

Emily swiped impatiently at her eyes. "I'll go get some Twizzlers from the vending machine." She got up from a picnic table outside the school cafeteria and entered through the door, disappearing around a corner.

As if on cue, Jinx appeared from around the other side of the building. She saw Jackson and nodded, her pink-tipped bangs flopping over her eyes. Swinging her bag up on the table, she blew a big breath up to get her bangs out of her eyes. Jackson could smell the perfume she swore she didn't wear, a musky scent.

"Where's our meal ticket?"

Jackson gave her what he hoped was his most disapproving stare. "*Emily*," he said.

Jinx grinned. "You say tomato . . ."

"She's going through a lot, you know. Just try to be nice, OK?"

Jinx shrugged and played with the corner of the *Fringe* patch she'd sewn onto her messenger bag. "Yeah, yeah, we all have it tough."

Just then Emily appeared at the door of the school, pushed, and walked slowly out.

"What does she think I am, a rabid dog?" Jinx asked.

Jackson had to hide a smile. Emily approached the picnic table and looked at Jinx and Jackson. She held her arm out straight in front of her. "I thought you might like these." The Twizzlers bag crinkled in her fingers. Her posture screamed "uncomfortable." Inwardly, Jackson cringed.

Jinx glared at Jackson—knowing who Emily had gotten her info from—then trained her gaze at Emily. "Well, sit down if you want to talk."

Emily took a seat across from them while Jinx snatched the Twizzlers.

Before Emily could say anything, Jinx said, "The fee is $400 with a $200 deposit. You pay us no matter what the outcome is. We can tell you if your place is haunted, but we don't guarantee we can get rid of them."

Emily looked from Jinx to Jackson, then back to Jinx. She glared at her. "What good does it do me to have you tell me my place is haunted? I *know* my place is haunted! I want you to get them out!"

Jackson was too startled to say anything. Jinx had just given him a big fat "I don't believe in you" vote when it came to getting rid of ghosts. Never mind that he actually didn't know how . . . she should still trust him!

"Just a minute, Emily," he said as the girl got up to move. "I need to talk to Jinx."

He grabbed Jinx by the upper arm—a move he knew she hated—and pulled her up, walking her to a shaded spot away from the picnic table.

"Dude, grab my arm again and I'll stick this Twizzler up your—"

Jackson cut her off. "What do you mean we can't make them go away?"

Jinx stared at him while the comprehension dawned on her. "Oh, Jackson, I didn't mean to say anything about you and your talents. It's just, we've never had to get rid of ghosts before."

Jackson glared. "We've never determined if there has *been* a ghost. So *you* may just suck at ghost *detection* too."

"It's just . . . I have all this equipment and you have . . . well, I don't know. You've never talked about it." Her voice trailed off. Jackson knew his face had darkened. He didn't say anything. She still should trust him.

Jinx finally sighed. "Well, come on. We'll say we can get rid of the things. But if we can't, you have to be the one to pay her back."

Jackson nodded and tried to playfully grab her upper arm again as they walked back to the picnic table.

"I *will* kung fu you," Jinx snarled. "Do not try me. I'm doing this whole thing as a favor to you anyway. And may I say again, I don't trust that girl."

Jackson snorted and said, "Yeah, yeah." He turned serious as they reached the table. Jinx flopped down opposite Emily and grabbed a Twizzler.

"OK," she said, taking one of her gigantic bites, "We'll get rid of the suckers for you. Guaranteed. Now, tell me why you think the place is haunted."

Emily's face relaxed and she almost smiled. She leaned in and said, "I'll tell you why I *know* it's haunted."

Jinx stared at her, affecting the most bored look Jackson knew she had. He elbowed her.

Emily went on. "Because the ghosts are trying to kill me."

CHAPTER 7

J inx swallowed her bite and tried to keep her bored expression up. *Overdramatic much?* she thought. But despite herself, she leaned in.

"Kill you how?" Jackson leaned in too. The boy was a sucker for these kinds of stories. Undoubtedly he was having white knight fantasies as Emily spoke.

Emily twisted the hem of her shirt, back and forth, back and forth. "Well, my parents just got divorced in May, and my mom moved to Seattle."

Jinx had to stop herself from rolling her eyes. Nowadays, it was worse if your parents were still together, in her view.

Emily went on as Jackson leaned in closer. "So we couldn't afford the house anymore, and my dad had to find an apartment."

"That must have been so hard for you," Jackson said.

Emily's eyes softened. "It really was because—"

Jinx didn't have time for a sob story. "So you got an apartment . . ."

Emily's big blue eyes trained on Jinx again. She nodded. "At the Falcon Perch apartments. It's kind of close to the school and near my dad's work, so it totally fit."

Jinx nodded impatiently.

"We didn't move until the end of July because we had to pack the house and everything," Emily continued. "So when we moved in, we were both really ready to get out of that house." Her eyes turned downward. "With all those memories . . . anyway, we both loved the apartment at first. Number 101. It's smaller, but it's got these cool old cupboards and like a laundry chute and even a door for an ice block. Plus there are the old radiators and the wood floors . . ."

Jinx rattled the Twizzlers package as loud as she could as she took another strand out. Boring, she thought. Jackson kicked her under the table. She frowned and kicked him back. Hard. Emily went on as if they weren't sitting in front of her. *Typical of her kind; it's all about her, her, her,* Jinx thought. Finally, she stopped rambling on about the old apartment and said something interesting.

"It started the third night. We were all unpacked, and I was just settling down to sleep. That's when I heard it."

"Heard what?" Jackson asked.

"The voice, coming from the wall."

Jinx couldn't help it—she snorted so loud she thought she might have broken something. "Like another tenant, maybe?"

Emily's face was white. "Not another tenant. This was inside the wall near my bed. And the voice whispered my name."

Jinx felt goose bumps form on her arms. She tried to shake them off—that could be explained away for a million different reasons.

"OK, what else?"

"That same night, after I heard the whisper, I told myself I was imagining it. So I went to the kitchen to get a drink of water, and all the cupboard doors were open." Emily looked at Jinx and Jackson, "Every single one."

Creepier, but there still could be a reason. Jinx nodded her on.

"From that night on, the things started getting worse. My dad has seen things happen too. Sometimes our furniture is moved in the middle of the night. One night I could feel something breathing on my neck. Noises happen constantly—banging, bumping, and even this loud wailing . . ." Tears started forming in her eyes. "The worst thing happened a couple of days ago, though. I went into the bathroom, and there was a note in my red lipstick on the mirror. It said, 'Get out.' And right underneath it, 'Or join us.'"

Jinx couldn't help it. She was seriously

creeped out. She noticed a shiver travel through Jackson too. Maybe, just maybe, this *was* a real haunting. To ease the tension, Jinx said, "Maybe you're being haunted by a girl group and they need a soprano. Can you dance?"

Jackson glared at her, but Emily gave a small smile. "I wish."

From out of her backpack, Jinx pulled out a notebook. Though she'd never tell Jackson, she had prepared for the meeting. If it was a real case, she wanted to be sure to do it right. She took out a pen and stared at Emily again.

"OK, let's go through these questions. Any cold spots in your place?" Emily nodded. "Where?" Jinx asked.

Emily looked taken aback by the question, then said, "It changes."

"OK. You've already said things have been moved, yes?"

Emily nodded again.

"Do you sense evil in the house? Feel an impending sense of doom?"

Emily teared up. Jackson put his hand on hers and quickly took it away.

"OK, finally, do you know of any people who have been killed in your apartment?" Jinx asked.

Emily's blue eyes widened. "I don't think so."

Jinx laughed. "You're getting haunted and you don't check the history of your place?" Under her breath she said to Jackson, "Amateur hour," then went on talking to Emily. "Well, here's the deal: we'll take the case."

Emily's eyes lit up, and Jinx could almost feel the happy energy wafting off Jackson. Jinx continued, "Bring the $200 tomorrow, and get your dad out of the house this Saturday somehow. I don't care how, but that's when we'll come over and stay the night and figure out what's going on." She looked sideways at Jackson and added, "And we'll do some research to see if there were any weird deaths at your place."

"Of course. Thank you, thank you!" Emily said. Jackson smiled big at her.

Jinx rolled her eyes. "Yeah, yeah. Don't thank us yet. In the meantime, you could be killed by a ghost."

Emily's face turned paler and Jinx smiled inwardly to herself. Maybe it would be fun working with her after all.

CHAPTER 8

Jinx tore around her basement, checking and double-checking all her equipment. She was excited for the upcoming night—Emily or no, the opportunity for a real-life ghost was too much.

Jackson bumped into her. She'd forgotten that he'd tagged along.

"Well, what can I do?" he asked.

Jinx lifted a blanket, looking for her EVP recorder. Typical of her, she'd put it somewhere and forgot where.

"I don't know," Jinx mumbled, "Learn how to get rid of ghosts?"

Jackson plunked down on the blanket she'd just lifted up.

"Jackson, my equipment could have been there!" He glared at her and she sighed. "I guess you could research the place, see if there have been any deaths . . ."

Jinx bent down and looked under the couch, yanking out a flip-flop she'd lost over a year ago. "Huh," she said and then threw it back under the couch. Meanwhile, Jackson's face split in a huge grin. "I'm on it." His smile vanished as quickly as it appeared. His shoulders slumped. "And then . . . I'll research how to get rid of the ghosts. Honestly, Jinx, you were right. I'm not sure how to go about doing it."

Jinx flopped down next to him. Jackson in pain was not an acceptable state.

"You'll figure it out," she said in her most soothing voice. Which, admittedly, wasn't very soothing. Jinx wondered what Jane would have done but then quickly dismissed the thought. Jane was no longer welcome. "I guess, start where anyone starts," she continued, "the Internet."

"Duh," Jackson said, "I've already done that. It's all advice from crazies. You know, talk to the ghosts, chant, imagine a white light. . . . Surely there's a better way."

Jinx shrugged. "I don't know. If someone said 'get out' to me, I probably wouldn't stay."

"Yeah, well, you're not the average person, Jinx."

Jinx glowed. She *wasn't* the average person. Not anymore.

"Let's go up to my room. I'll set things up on the laptop, and you can research on my desk computer."

Jackson nodded and they tromped upstairs. On the way up, Jackson stopped at the kitchen and grabbed a soda and a fistful of Oreos. Jinx just shook her head. He was always eating. Then she grabbed a soda too.

As Jackson sat on the *Ikea* chair in her room, Jinx heard the downstairs door open and knew her mom was home.

She said to Jackson, "We also have to figure out how I can get away with a sleepover."

"*We?*" He smiled big and threw an Oreo into his mouth. Jinx tossed a pillow at him, missing by a mile. Jackson chuckled to himself and fired up the computer.

"I'm home!" her mother called. Jinx answered back, "Hey, Mom."

She appeared in the doorway. "What are you kids doing today? Homework?"

Jinx said, "Uh, yeah," and huffed at the interruption.

Jackson grinned. "Hey, Mrs. W."

Jinx's mom smiled, her eyes crinkling up at the corners. Jinx would never tell her, but she thought her mom was beautiful. Long red hair, green eyes, and a face that could pass for twenty-five. She was still super old but younger than other moms anyway.

"Hey, Jackson, how are you?" Her eyes squinted. Jinx knew she was always concerned about Jackson. She liked that about her mom.

He shrugged. "Good."

Jinx's mom said, "OK, well, you guys don't

work too hard." And then she disappeared.

"Finally." Jinx opened her laptop and started typing up the plan. Only, she didn't know what to write. She'd never had to write a plan before. She glanced at Jackson, who was engrossed at the desk computer. Then she looked back at the blinking cursor on her screen. Sitting up, she said, "What are you finding?"

Jackson looked at her. "I just started! It's been like two seconds since your mom left. What, you have no preparation you can do?"

Jinx flopped back down. "As if. I have the hard job. I just wanted to make sure you aren't screwing up." She'd never say this to Jackson, but she *did* think she had the hard job. Who cared if they got rid of ghosts? She had given the job to him because she truly didn't care about that part. Making contact, *recording* contact—that was the fun stuff. But he didn't need to know that.

Jinx continued to look at the blinking cursor. How to organize the night? she wondered. Just when she thought the cursor would actually drive her insane, Jackson piped up.

"So you know how I just started the search? Well, Falcon Perch apartments is all over the place on the Web. As in, all over in the haunted section."

Jinx's pulse shot up. She sat up in bed again. "Really?"

Jackson nodded, still staring at the screen. Then he looked at her. "But that's not all. The apartment that keeps coming up? Apartment 101."

CHAPTER 9

Jackson could hardly believe it. Not only was the apartment building haunted, but the most haunted apartment was the one Emily lived in. He felt a chill run through him like cold water down his neck.

He and Jinx shared a smile. Jackson knew she was thinking the same thing: this could actually be real.

He turned back to the page. "It says right here that the management has been in trouble because of 'strange occurrences' in that apartment. But the government doesn't think ghosts are a viable excuse . . ."

Jinx scooted to the edge of the bed and squinted at the computer. "Is that a newspaper article?"

"Yeah, from one of the freebies that coffee shops have? The *Jar*. It's always doing 'exposés' about things. Falcon Perch has been exposed." He wriggled his eyebrows at her.

Jinx leaned in further. "When was it published? Is this pretty recent?"

Jackson scrolled back to the top of the article. "Yeah, about two months ago."

Jinx's eyes lit up. "Jackson, we might actually have a haunting! Emily might not be full of crap!"

I could've told you that, Jackson thought. No way would Emily look like such a mess unless something bad was going on.

But Jinx was on to something else. "OK, can you find out if anyone died in there?"

Jackson skimmed the article. "Well, according to Earl, the caretaker . . ." He looked at Jinx. "Are people still named Earl?" Jinx bumped into him so he went on. "A couple did die in the apartment. Evidently a murder-suicide." He sat back. "Whoa. That's heavy."

Jinx twisted her lip and stared intently at the computer. "I wonder if there's a way we can confirm that."

Jackson leaned forward again. "My mom works for the city. Maybe she can call up the records or something."

"Do you think that's a good idea? I mean, won't she get suspicious if you ask her that stuff and then go away for a night?"

Jackson shrugged. "She won't care—I'm going to tell her the truth about what we're doing."

Jinx shook her head. "So different to be a boy . . . anyway, ask her. We have three more days until Saturday. We should know what we're dealing with here."

"And the plan?" Jackson said.

Jinx flopped back on the bed and mumbled, "Will you help me with it?"

Jackson smiled slightly. He knew how hard it was for her to ask for help. "What was that?" he asked, putting on what he hoped was his most innocent expression.

A little louder, Jinx mumbled, "Help me?"

Jackson grinned openly and said, "I still didn't hear you."

Sitting straight up, Jinx yelled, "Will you help me with it already!?"

"Well, all you had to do was ask."

She slung an Oreo at him and he laughed. Sometimes it was good to remind her that they had a partnership, not just a Jinxship.

"OK, where should we start?"

Four hours later, Jackson and Jinx sat back and admired their handiwork. The plan had taken a while to get together, but they had it. Jackson's mind already was jumping ahead, though, to the research he would do at home. He needed to find out how to get rid of ghosts, yes. But also, he needed to find something out that was way more important, something Jinx would never understand. Would she? He studied her while she looked at the paper with the plan.

His heart thudded. What would she say if he told her? She was his best friend. Surely she'd understand . . . but Jackson *wasn't* so sure.

She could be way harsh. What would she say if he told her he was looking for a way to bring ghosts to *him*?

Suddenly, Jinx looked up at him. "What? Did your face get stuck?"

Jackson shook off the urge to tell her and pushed her shoulder. "So—we have a plan, and now we just need to execute it, huh?"

Jinx nodded. "And then we come back here and check out the equipment readings. After that, it's getting-rid-of-ghosts time."

She twisted her lip, her telltale sign of anxiety. She stood up and walked around the room, touching her Pixies poster. Though she'd never told him, Jackson knew it was for good luck. For such a budding scientist and tech geek, Jinx had a lot of superstitions.

"Now all we have to do is convince my parents that I'm staying somewhere over night." She looked up at Jackson, searching his face. "I mean, you were right. I don't have any friends. All I have is you."

All Jackson could do was give her a hug.

CHAPTER 10

So, Jinx thought, *this is the downside of
alienating everyone. Not having friends . . .*

Jackson had left for dinner, and Jinx
could smell the smells of spaghetti night
coming from her family's kitchen. The
clatter of dishes meant her dad was home,
making his famous spaghetti sauce. Garlic
smell wafted to her nose, and her stomach
growled. *Good thing I don't have a boyfriend to
kiss*, she thought. Tonight would be a perfect
time to try to fool her parents—spaghetti

night almost always guaranteed parental good moods.

She squared her shoulders and then stomped down the stairs in her usual fashion. She popped her head into the kitchen.

As if reading from a script, her mother said the usual, "Do you have to come down the stairs like a herd of elephants?"

Jinx shot back her typical, "Sorry, I forgot. Guess I'm not a herd of elephants, then." She batted her eyelashes.

"Hey, pumpkin!" her dad said from the stove. He stirred deep in a pot, and his face was bright red, hair sticking up. "How was the asylum today?"

Jinx rolled her eyes. He always called school the asylum. "Fine," she said and grabbed a piece of garlic bread to munch on. Before she could get it to her mouth, someone slapped it away, and it fell to the floor. She looked up in rage. Slime. Of course.

"Look what you did, dingleberry!"

"Mom!" her brother yelled. "Jane called me dingleberry!"

"He knocked that piece of bread on the floor!"

Her mom sighed a sigh so long that Jinx wondered how she had any breath left. And then the worst thing happened. Jinx saw her mom's mood change, like thunderclouds rolling in. She needed to fix it, fast.

Quickly, Jinx said, "Mom, did you get your hair cut?"

Her mother touched her hair and then shook her head. "No, why?"

"It just looks really good, that's all." Jinx tried hard to keep an innocent look on her face.

Her mother frowned. "Jane, regardless of how my hair looks, you have to be nice to your brother."

Jinx growled. She was always supposed to be nice to her brother, yet her brother never had to be nice to her. Jinx would never understand how that passed for fair.

She grabbed another piece of garlic bread and bit into it, then flopped down for dinner. Now *she* was in a bad mood. She sat at her chair, chewing and glaring angrily at her brother. He stuck his tongue out at her when her parents' backs were turned.

Jinx needed to recalibrate. How was she going to approach her parents? So far it hadn't gone so well.

Her dad set down the steaming pot and the glorious smell of spaghetti sauce took over the kitchen. Her mom plunked down the spaghetti, Parmesan, and red pepper flakes. Finally, her dad poured the water and the whole family sat down for dinner.

Jinx looked at each of her parents, trying to gauge expressions. Sure enough, spaghetti night had everyone slurping and snorfling happily. Even Slime had a big smile on his face.

Twirling her fork in the mound of spaghetti on her plate, Jinx said, "Shaun, will you pass me the red pepper?"

Her brother stared at her, mouth open, showing half-chewed spaghetti. Both of her parents looked at her in confusion. Maybe calling her brother by his real name was a step too far.

Her brother handed her the red pepper slowly, as if he was afraid she would bite. She snatched it out of his hand and said, "Took you long enough, Slime." The whole table seemed to relax, and pretty soon, the only sound was of forks scraping and clanking on plates.

With a strand of spaghetti twirled on her fork, Jinx said, "So I've been invited to a slumber party on Saturday night."

Her mother actually dropped her fork, and her dad choked a little. Slime snorted. "Yeah, right!"

Jinx threw a piece of garlic bread at him. "Shut it, dingleberry!"

"Jane!" her mom said, then added, "And, Shaun, don't taunt your sister."

Her dad drank a huge gulp of water and set the glass down. "That's great, honey! Who's the girl?"

Jinx sighed internally. She'd decided that the easiest thing to do was to tell the truth. "Her name is Emily. She lives in the Falcon Perch apartments."

Her mom stared at her until Jinx said, "What?!"

Quickly, her mother shook her head.

"Nothing, honey. I think it's great. You haven't had a girlfriend since . . . um . . ." She put her finger to her mouth. After a big pause, she said, "a while ago."

Jinx twirled her fork into her spaghetti. She mumbled, "Don't say girlfriend, Mom. That sounds so old." She stared at her plate and pushed the spaghetti around. Though she'd never admit it, she was also a little surprised that she didn't have any friends who were girls. Briefly, she wondered why. Then she remembered: they all sucked.

Sitting up straighter, she said, "So can I go?"

Her mom and dad looked at each other. Her mom gave a little shrug, and her dad said, "Sure!"

Jinx sat back and put a giant fork full of spaghetti in her mouth. Well, she wasn't sure how she felt about her parents being so excited she had a female friend, but she'd gotten her way. And pretty easily too. Come Saturday night, she would be knee-deep in ghosts. A shiver of excitement shot through her. She had a feeling this would change everything.

CHAPTER 11

The next three days at school dragged by for Jackson. He only got more nervous as the weekend drew nearer. By Friday, even Jinx, who really only thought of herself, noticed his moods.

"Seriously, Jackson, go dunk your head in water or something. Snap out of it!"

Jackson glared at her. "Snap out of what?" But he knew exactly what she was talking about—he'd snapped at everything she'd said.

They were sitting at the picnic tables outside the school, going over the plan one more time.

Jinx leaned in. "Did you find anything that sounded like real ghost-banishing techniques?"

Jackson snapped, "I'm looking! Anyway, I have the hard part of this whole deal." He moved away from her, and Jinx snapped her notebook closed.

"All right, that's it. I'll see you tomorrow. Sleep this mood off, dude. You're being a real—"

"Sorry, sorry. I just . . . I can't find anything that doesn't involve crystals and stuff. I don't want to end up having to do some stupid ritual and hoping it works." He didn't tell her the real reason he was upset—he couldn't find anything, not one thing, on how to bring a ghost back.

Jinx, who was half on and half off of the picnic table bench, sat back down. Her brown eyes softened, and she almost touched his hand, then moved to play with her *Fringe* patch.

"Look, we don't even know if we're dealing with a ghost yet," she said. "You may have nothing to get rid of."

"Yeah, but from what Emily said, it's pretty bad."

Jinx snorted. "And I'm sure she's totally reliable."

"Jinx, not everybody is as bad as you think, you know."

Jinx stood up and swung her backpack onto her shoulders. "I'll believe it when I see it. I wish there was an 'Intention-meter' like the EMF monitor I have."

Jackson laughed. "*Or* you could just trust people."

Jinx spread her hands in a what-are-you-gonna-do? gesture, and Jackson felt his mood begin to lighten.

They walked to the old Impala that used to be his brother's. Jinx got in and said, "OK, one more time."

Jackson nodded and started, "So we go over around eleven and set up the equipment."

"I'll set up the EVP recorder and the EMF sensor in the places where Emily said there was the most activity."

Jackson's brow crinkled. "Explain to me

what those are again?"

Jinx sighed but Jackson knew it was just for show. She liked nothing better than to take him through the details of her tech-head geek equipment.

"EVP stands for 'electronic voice phenomena' and is used to record any voices that may be struggling to speak," she said. "So, like, if a ghost isn't that strong and his voice comes through the static in a radio or something." Jackson nodded and tried to look interested, but he had to work at it. He kind of regretted asking.

Jinx went on. "EMF stands for 'electromagnetic field' sensor. That will let us know if there are any electromagnetic changes in the atmosphere, which means a ghost's nearby. Also, mine has a temperature gauge, so we can tell if the temperature goes way down. Finally," she said, practically bouncing in the seat, "we'll set up the camera in the kitchen-slash-living room."

"Then we'll all go to Emily's room and hang out!" Jackson finished up.

Jinx elbowed him. *"Right.* Then we sit and ask if the ghost wants to contact us. Maybe we should bring magnets or something. . . ."

Jackson didn't ask her to elaborate. He only understood about a third of what Jinx said most of the time. He did ask, "So if there are ghosts there, then . . .?"

"Then we tell Emily we'll come back another night to get rid of the ghosts," Jinx finished. She hesitated and then said slowly to Jackson, "I think we should have one camera that we don't tell Emily about. Right in the same area."

Jackson turned onto their block and pulled into Jinx's driveway. He could feel anger rising up in him. He thought he knew the answer, but he asked anyway: "Why?"

Jinx hugged her bag closer on her lap. "I just want you to consider the possibility. . ." Jackson shook his head, but she said louder, "the *possibility* that Emily may be lying."

Jackson's bad mood returned with a vengeance. Why couldn't she for once think about someone else besides herself? Emily was in *pain.* Anyone with eyeballs could see that. Sometimes being Jinx's friend was near impossible. He could hear his voice come out louder than he meant it to. "Why would she do that, Jinx? Tell me, *why*?"

Jinx just shrugged and tightened her lips, staring out the windshield.

Jackson went on. "Listen, I know Emily. She looks horrible, and she keeps crying in the hallway. Do you think she would let people see her like that if something wasn't truly wrong? Even if you don't trust her, Jinx, I need you to trust *me*." He shifted angrily into reverse, keeping his foot on the brake.

The silence settled in the car, thick. Just when Jackson thought he couldn't take any more, Jinx said, "OK."

Jackson put the car in park and looked at her. "OK?"

Jinx looked at him with a half smile. "OK. I trust you."

Jackson was flooded with happiness. He knew what a step it was for Jinx to let go a little bit. He punched her shoulder lightly. "About time."

She punched him in the shoulder hard. "Dingus." She opened the door and got out, then leaned back in and said, "Tomorrow night, eleven. I'll meet you at Emily's?" Jackson nodded. Jinx went on, "Remember, park far away. My parents know your car."

He smiled at her and said, "Trust me."

Jinx snorted. "Once a day is enough."

Jackson chuckled to himself as he pulled out of the driveway.

CHAPTER 12

Jinx literally shook with excitement all the way to Emily's. Her dad kept asking her questions, but Jinx could hardly think above the pounding of her heart. Sure, she hated Emily with the passion of a thousand white-hot suns—and she thought there was a chance the girl was lying about everything—but the idea of a real ghost hunt had her bouncing off the walls.

She sprinted out of the van with bag full of equipment bouncing against her hip, and barely heard her dad yell, "Have a good time, sweetie!" He hadn't even asked why she was going over so late. Her parents were just so happy that she had a friend that they would have let her do about anything. She flopped her hand at her dad, and he drove away.

Jinx stared at the list of tenants on the outside door. Did she remember Emily's last name? Was Jackson inside already? Just as she had the thought, someone grabbed her sides and squeezed. A loud "boo!" echoed in her ear, and she heard a girly scream come out of her mouth.

Whirling around, Jinx saw Jackson doubled over with laughter. She was furious—she hadn't known her scream was so girly. She pushed him, and he barely kept his balance.

Straightening up, he wiped his eyes. "Sorry, Jinx, it's just I thought I heard a girl for a second with that scream."

"Come on," Jinx snapped. "Let's go."

They turned around, and both of them jumped back. Staring at them through the glass door to the building was an impossibly skinny man in a janitor's uniform. His sunken cheeks and the dark circles under his eyes gave Jinx a shiver. The man was just creepy.

He opened the door slowly, and the creak echoed off the brick walls. Staring at them, he asked, "Well, are you coming in?"

Jinx and Jackson looked at each other. "Are you Emily's dad?" Jinx said.

"Who?" the skinny man replied. "No, I'm the caretaker. Which apartment you going to?"

Jackson answered, "Apartment 101."

The man almost let the door shut, like he'd been shocked, but caught it just in time. With a big swallow, he said, "I wouldn't go in there, if I were you."

Jinx said, "Why?"

The man waved them in, and Jinx and Jackson walked through the door.

Visibly shaking, the man answered Jinx: "No reason. Faulty pipes." With that, he ran down the stairs to the basement.

After a beat, Jackson said, "Whoa."

Jinx nodded and looked at him with huge eyes. "I know. This is awesome!" They walked up the stairs and reached the apartment.

"Well, this is it," Jackson said, then knocked.

Emily answered the door as if she'd been standing right behind it. Her hair was even stringier, and the dark circles under her eyes had grown. "Thank god you're here. It's gotten worse."

With fresh tears in her eyes, she slid her sleeve up. An angry red cut darkened her pale skin.

CHAPTER 13

Jackson's stomach clenched. Anger coursed through him—he would get rid of these things if it was the last thing he did. He strode in, giving Emily a big hug. "We'll fix this." She buried her head in his shoulder, and he could feel the wet tears on his shirt. His resolve strengthened, and he said, "Jinx, do you want to set up the equipment?"

Jinx saluted him and said, "Aye, Captain!" Sarcasm dripped from her voice. He ignored it and said to Emily, "Tell us what happened."

Emily took a shuddery breath. "I was lying in bed and I heard the voice in the kitchen again and when I walked out to see if it was my dad, something slashed me. It happened right before you came."

Jackson sat her down on the couch. "So in our research, we found that the kitchen and this living room is where something did actually happen."

Emily's eyes widened. "What?"

Jackson met Jinx's eyes as she set up the camera in the corner. "Well, there was a murder-suicide here, Emily. About fifteen years ago. Right in this very place."

A shudder ran through Emily, and she looked down. "Actually," she said, "that makes me feel a little better. At least I know why these things might be happening."

Jackson nodded and looked back at Jinx. She was placing letter magnets on the refrigerator. He noticed a teddy bear sitting in the corner.

"What are those things?" He was slightly annoyed that she forgot to mention this part to him.

"Oh, just extra things I thought about today. The magnets are in case the ghost has a message for us, and the teddy bear is something light for it to throw." She kept her eyes down.

She's acting weird, Jackson thought. He shrugged it off.

Turning back to Emily, he said, "Are you ready for this?"

"More than ready," she replied. "I want this to stop."

Jinx called from the corner, her eyes already fixed on her EMF sensor. "All systems are go. Now we just wait." Emily sank into the couch and Jackson slumped in his chair.

A couple of hours later, Jinx sprang up. Emily had gone into her bedroom, so exhausted she couldn't keep her eyes open. Jackson had been dozing on the couch. He heard the gasp and sat up sleepily, checking his watch. 1:12 a.m.

"What?" he said.

Jinx's face was pale, and he could see the EMF sensor in front of her blinking a bright red.

"Are the hairs on your arm standing up?"

she asked.

Jackson checked his arm—yep. He looked in wonder at Jinx.

She nodded. "We're not alone."

Jackson shivered. The temperature in the room had dropped significantly. He started to whisper, though he didn't know why. "What should we do?"

Jinx swallowed. "Talk to it?"

He nodded and willed his voice to work. After all, this was the plan. Funny how in the moment, though, both he and Jinx almost forgot what they were going to do.

Jackson cleared his throat and said, "Hello?"

Jinx said, louder, "If you're out there, will you say something?"

Jackson remembered something and leaned toward her. "Jinx, the paper said the clocks stopped at 1:15. Maybe that's when everything happened." They both looked at the clock. The temperature dropped another degree, and static rippled through the air.

At that moment, the clock on the stove flipped over to 1:15.

CHAPTER 14

Jinx felt something rumble through the room. She began to shake and moved closer to Jackson.

"Do you feel that?" she whispered.

Jackson nodded. When Jinx glanced at him, his face had turned bright white. As if he'd seen a ghost.

All of a sudden, the TV in the corner switched on. Jinx jumped so hard she bumped into Jackson. Static crackled on the screen, and the bright light flickered around the room like a living thing.

"I think they're here," Jackson said.

Jinx shivered. Then she remembered the EVP recorder. She crawled toward it and checked to make sure the green light was on. Check—it was recording. That meant something was talking.

Out of the static, Jinx thought she heard a long moan. Jackson tensed up beside her.

"What do we do?" he whispered to her.

Jinx half shrugged, her eyes fixed on the TV screen. "Keep talking to them?"

"We want to know why you're here," Jackson said into the air. "Why do you stay in this apartment?" His shaky voice floated around the room.

Silence followed his question. Jinx had just started to relax when a door slammed so hard elsewhere in the apartment that the pictures on the wall shook.

Jinx looked wide-eyed at Jackson, and Jackson looked back. They said, at the same time, "Emily."

They raced to Emily's room. Jackson tried the handle, but it wouldn't budge.

"Emily!" he called.

From the other side of the door, Jinx heard a muffled sound. She could make out the word *help*, she thought, but not much else.

Jackson jiggled the handle again, a bead of sweat dripping down the side of his face. "Emily! Are you OK? Can you answer?"

Jinx pounded on the door, and Jinx kicked at it. They both yelled, "Emily," over and over but heard nothing. Then suddenly, the door gave way, and Jinx and Jackson tumbled through.

Emily stood above them. "It cut me again!" Her body began trembling with sobs. She showed them an angry red streak above the first cut.

As Jinx and Jackson scrambled up, Jinx asked, "What did it cut you with?" She looked wildly around the room, waiting for a knife or some other sharp instrument to stab her.

A voice boomed through the apartment: "Get out!"

All three of them ducked and grabbed onto one another.

"That's the loudest it's ever spoken," Emily said. "I think you've made it mad." A trickle of blood from Emily's arm dripped on the floor.

Just then, the sound of slamming cupboard doors filled the apartment. *Slam, slam, slam,* one after another, faster and faster, so loud that Jinx had to cover her ears. At the same time, the radio in Emily's room flipped on. New voices traveled through the apartment, so loud that all three of them covered their ears and ducked.

And then it stopped.

Jinx could hear the ticking of Jackson's watch in the quiet room. And the beats of her own pounding heart. Her arms were covered in goose bumps, and she was sweating, breathing hard.

A look at Emily and Jackson told her they all felt the same way.

Finally, Jackson spoke. "Do you think it's gone?"

Emily nodded. "It normally only lasts a little bit. But I'm usually too scared to go back to sleep."

Jinx gathered herself and took a deep breath. "Well, let's go out to the living room, and I'll gather up the equipment."

The three walked out of the room, Jinx in the lead. They all stopped in sync. On the refrigerator, the magnets had arranged themselves to spell out: YOU WL DIE NXT.

Jinx looked at Emily and Jackson. "Well. I'd say your place is haunted."

CHAPTER 15

The next day, Jackson could hardly believe everything that had happened the night before. Emily was not joking. Maybe Jinx would finally trust other people now. He honestly didn't know how Emily could have lived with that level of fear for so long.

Just as important, though, Jackson had gotten his first experience with ghosts! Psychotic, murderous ghosts, yes, but ghosts. And his biggest question, the one he hadn't even allowed himself to ask, was answered.

Ghosts were real.

That meant he might be able to see his dad again.

Just the thought made his heart leap. What if he could say one more thing to his dad? Just one more "I love you"? The thought almost brought tears to his eyes.

Alone in his room, he kept looking at his phone. He and Jinx had spent the rest of the evening at Emily's, eyes wide open. Neither of them had gotten any sleep. They both went home to nap. Jackson had been up for three hours since then, but he knew Jinx would take longer.

He checked the clock. 3:55. He'd told his friends he'd meet them for a game of ultimate Frisbee at 4:30. If Jinx didn't call soon, he'd have to go. And the girl could sleep for days.

Finally, at 4:10, he could wait no longer. He texted Jinx, "When you get your lazy butt up, call me. I'll be at ultimate game until 6." Then he hustled down the stairs, grabbing a bottle of water from the fridge before stepping outside.

Luckily, the park was only a ten-minute walk. Jackson got there just in time. Two of the guys were late, but that was normal.

He jogged up to the circle where the guys were throwing the Frisbee back and forth, talking to Joe and Brian, fellow football teammates.

Finally, the other boys showed up and smacked each other's shoulders hello. As they walked to the field, Jackson heard Joe say to Travis, one of the guys who showed up late, "So you were out with Emily last night? Thanks for dogging us, man." He gave him a shove.

Jackson tried to look over without attracting Travis's attention. Travis glanced at Jackson for a second, then said, "No, man, I stayed home."

Joe's face registered confusion. "I thought you said you were hanging with Emily last night? I mean, no worries, we're used to you ditching us for your girlfriend . . ." He smiled and pushed Travis again. Travis half smiled and glanced back at Jackson.

As they walked, Jackson wondered: Why was Travis acting so strange? Come to think of it, where was he with this whole haunting thing? Shouldn't he be in the loop, if he and Emily were dating? Something was definitely up.

Just then, his phone vibrated near the top of his bag. He pulled it out and checked the text. It was from Jinx: "Come over right away. Things aren't what they seem."

He looked up from his phone and said, "Hey guys, I have to bail. Something just came up."

CHAPTER 16

J inx tapped the Pixies poster over and
over again. How was she going to tell
Jackson what she had found? Or worse, the
way she had found it?

She twisted her lip and took a lap around
the room. This was not good—one instance
when she wished she hadn't been right.

Slumping back down into her hair, she started
watching the video on her computer screen again.
She couldn't believe it. Jackson would be so hurt.
And she would be the messenger.

She sat straight up. Maybe she didn't have to be the messenger. Maybe he could find out for himself.

Just then, the front door opened and she heard her name yelled out. Jackson never knocked. From downstairs a soda can popped and hissed and some sort of bag crinkled loudly. He would be up the stairs soon.

He stood in her doorway munching chips. Through a mouthful, he said, "So what's with the cryptic message?"

Jinx thought fast. "We need to do another night at Emily's."

Jackson chewed thoughtfully. "Why?"

"Some of the data was skewed," Jinx said. "We need to redo some things for evidence's sake."

Jackson flopped on her bed. "Evidence? Like there wasn't a ghost? You were there, right?"

He put his legs up on Jinx's computer desk, and she pushed them off, angry. "We need to be sure—to have documentation." She spoke with exaggerated slowness.

Jackson's eyes narrowed. "Jinx, there were ghosts there. We both saw, both felt it."

Jinx shrugged. She had no idea why he was getting so defensive. "Look, the equipment bugged out. You can come or not. I'll call Emily."

Jackson rolled his eyes. "Yeah, right. I'll come with you, but this time set up your equipment right."

Jinx had to fight the urge to punch him. She almost wished she could tell him what she found. Show him the video the teddy bear camera had captured. But she told him she'd trust him, and she had betrayed him by bringing in the secret teddy cam. There was no way around it.

He got up and said, "I'll call Emily about tonight. I think her dad is out of town through Tuesday. What are you going to tell your parents?"

Jinx sighed. "Test? They're so happy I have a 'friend' they'll pretty much let me do anything."

Jackson snorted. "Handy. Same time? Hopefully Emily will be up for it."

Jinx nodded. She hoped that Jackson would talk to her again once the night was over.

CHAPTER 17

Jinx was acting weird, no doubt about it. But so was Jackson—he wasn't sure why he felt the need to keep the information about Emily and Travis a secret, but he did. And he felt bad about it. Jinx would never lie to him. But something fishy was definitely going on, and Jinx didn't need any more reasons to be suspicious.

His conversation with Emily went well. She was resistant to another night ghost-watching at first but then quickly agreed when Jackson mentioned evidence. She'd said something about needing to convince her dad. But, Jackson wondered, hadn't these things been happening when he was there?

He put everything aside and decided that tonight he'd try anything to get rid of the ghosts, as silly as some of the suggestions he'd seen online were. He packed crystals, a book of chants, and a bundle of sage that was supposed to work as a "smudge stick" to "clean the energy of the apartment."

Finally, 10:45 came around, and he went to pick up Jinx—she'd told her parents he would drive her to her "friend's" house. Just like earlier, when Jinx got in the car, she acted cagey and guarded, but Jackson chalked it up to nerves. The night before had been terrifying.

When they got to Emily's, she was waiting at the door to the outside. "Can you get rid of them tonight after you gather evidence?" she asked Jackson.

Jackson nodded. "I think so." They three of them started to walk up the stairs to Emily's apartment. He thought he heard Jinx let out a little laugh. When Jackson glanced at her, she was staring at Emily with, if possible, more loathing than before. She saw him looking and rearranged her expression to neutral.

In the apartment, Jinx set up all the equipment. Everything went into the same place, including the silly teddy bear and the magnet letters she'd brought before. He shrugged it off. Everything looked set up the exact same way as the previous night, but Jackson figured he just didn't know the ins and outs of the equipment like Jinx did. They settled on the couch to wait. Jinx barely said a word. Even Emily noticed and looked nervously at her from time to time.

At 12:30, Emily went into her bedroom. Jackson settled in the chair. He could feel Jinx looking at him, but he was just too tired to ask why. Before he knew it, he began to doze off. Thoughts of his dad and ghosts and crystals and teddy bears swirled in his head, and pretty soon he was enveloped in the deep, dark waters of sleep.

Jackson woke up fast to the sound of a door slamming. He bolted upright, looking around the room in confusion. For some reason, Jinx was on the floor, sticking her fingers in a narrow gap between the room's floorboards and the wall. She looked at him and said nonchalantly, "Guess we should go to Emily's room."

But Jackson was already on his feet, racing to the room again. Why did it seem like a good idea for her to sleep there again? He saw the clock on the stove: 1:15.

He got to the door and pounded on it. He looked back and saw Jinx sauntering toward him. "Will you help me, please?" he hissed.

Her lips formed a frown, and she hurried up just a little bit. When she got to the door, she knocked listlessly. "Open the door, Emily," she said in a bored voice.

The door opened inward, as it had done the night before.

Emily stood there again, another slash on her wrist—now there were three angry cuts. Jackson grabbed her arm and said, "Again?"

Jinx stepped quickly to his side. She whispered to him, "Go check the kitchen. Now!"

Jackson looked at her in confusion. Her eyes were so intense, burning. He knew that look. This was important.

He said, "I'll be right back, Emily."

Panicked, Emily cried, "Don't leave me!"

The same voice from the night before said, "Get out," the echo reverberating around the apartment.

Jinx grabbed Jackson's arm and pushed him toward the kitchen, but Emily grabbed his other arm, pleading with her eyes.

"Please, please, please don't leave me!"

With a last "sorry" look to Emily, Jackson hurried out of the room.

CHAPTER 18

Jinx let out a breath she didn't know she'd been holding. Jackson chose to trust her. And now the jig was up.

She turned to Emily, who watched Jackson walk out the door. Emily's expression was hopeless. She whirled to Jinx, her face contorting in anger.

"You," was all she could say.

Jinx could give as good as she could get. She hardened her eyes and narrowed them. "It's over, Emily. Your little trick didn't work."

Emily glared at Jinx. "So, you're a freak *and* a jerk?"

Jinx snorted. "I'm a jerk because I found out you've been lying this whole time?"

Emily walked over and flopped onto her bed, her shoulders sagging. The fight had left her. Distantly, Jackson's voice carried through the apartment: "What the—?" He'd found Travis in the kitchen, Jinx knew.

Emily shook her head sadly. "All you had to do was just say there were ghosts in the apartment. Why couldn't you have just done that? How did you know, anyway?"

Jinx sat on the bed next to her, her loathing overshadowed by her curiosity. "Why did you do this?" she asked. "Why go through all this work? Were you doing this to make fun of me?"

"No offense, Jinx," Emily replied, "but I couldn't have cared less about you until this year." Jinx's back stiffened. They were all the same, these people. Had nothing changed since middle school?

"But then my parents got divorced. My dad had to move out to this apartment. . . . I

Googled it and found out about the murder and the haunting. It just clicked to contact you."

"But why?" Jinx asked. She couldn't seem to connect the dots. Off in the kitchen, she could hear Travis and Jackson talking. Leave it to Jackson to be calm and reasonable about everything. Jinx, though, felt furious. How could she be this girl's fool? She calmed herself long enough for an answer.

Emily sighed, picking at the bedcover in front of her. The threads were coming loose. Jinx could tell that the quilt was homemade. By someone really talented—it was beautiful. Emily saw her looking at it and said, "My mom made this. She's an amazing sewer. She even started designing clothes a year or two ago."

Emily got up and went to her closet, pulling out a skirt and a sweater. Jinx could see the quality in the fabric and design, and how expensive the clothes looked. Probably not something she would wear, but . . .

"This is my mom's design," Emily said.

Jinx nodded, then moved her hand in a go-on motion. "Annnd?"

"And she got really successful. Now she doesn't have time for me and my dad."

Jinx couldn't help it. Her eyes softened, and she relaxed a little bit. She couldn't even imagine one of her parents checking out. Emily sat back down on the bed and unraveled some more of the quilt thread. "I thought, if my mom thought we were in danger, she'd let us come home," she went on. "Both of us."

A tear slipped down her face. This girl was a good actor, Jinx thought, but she was sure there was real pain here. Maybe Jackson was right about one thing.

Jinx put her hand out to pat Emily's shoulder but just couldn't do it and ended up smoothing her hand along the quilt too. Emily looked up at her curiously, but Jinx turned away and cleared her throat.

"So you asked Travis to help, huh?"

Emily nodded. "He's been so great. When all this stuff happened, he was really there for me."

Jinx sighed. They were both quiet for a moment. The only sounds were the soft mumbling in the kitchen and Emily's occasional sniff.

Finally, Jinx said, "Look, I'm not one for advice, but this seems like a really extreme way to get your mom's attention. Maybe if you just talk to her . . . you know, tell her you miss her, she'll listen? What if she doesn't know you feel that way?"

After a beat, Emily said, "I guess I actually haven't told her I feel like I'm a nuisance."

Jinx nodded. "It'll be easier than faking a ghost."

Both girls chuckled softly, and Jinx stood up. "Well, time to talk to Jackson." Emily nodded and got up too.

Jinx said, "Oh, and by the way. You still owe us the $200."

She could only be so nice, after all.

CHAPTER 19

Three days later, Jackson and Jinx sat in Jinx's basement, watching *Ghost Hunters*. Jinx munched on her Twizzlers as usual, commenting on the various pieces of equipment on-screen and ways to save up to get some of it herself. And also how "amateurish" the *Ghost Hunters* were. Jackson had to laugh—one foray into "professional" ghost hunting and Jinx was an expert.

After Jackson discovered Travis in the kitchen rearranging the magnetic letters on the refrigerator, he knew they'd been had. He couldn't believe that Jinx had been right—Emily had been lying the whole time. Travis told Jackson about the divorce and Emily's desperate attempt to get her parents back together. Jackson could see why she did it. But the whole thing made him sad nonetheless. He was surprised, though, that Jinx hadn't gloated. Not even an "I told you so." Maybe she thought he was upset enough. And the truth was, Jackson *was* really sad. Because Emily's lying didn't just mean that he had misplaced his faith in people. It meant that the ghosts weren't real.

It meant that he might never see his father again.

He pushed the thought aside and tried to concentrate on the future, trying to will the depression away. He and Jinx would just have to find another case like this one. And hopefully, Jinx wouldn't find out that some client's boyfriend was the ghost.

He sat up suddenly. How had Jinx found out? He looked at her.

"Wha?" she said, mid-bite, her eyebrows coming together in confusion.

"How did you know that Travis would be in the kitchen that night at Emily's?" Jackson asked.

Jinx swallowed her Twizzler and looked away. She shrugged. "Women's intuition."

"Jane Marie Wright. What are you hiding from me?"

Jinx glared her meanest glare at him, but Jackson refused to look away. "Don't. Ever. Call. Me. That." she said.

He stared at her. "How did you know?"

"It was nothing. Just an extra step I did. . . ." She twisted her lip and pretended to look at something on the couch.

"*Jinx*." Jackson was getting nervous. What had she done? After he'd asked her to trust him . . .

Jinx sighed and sat down next to him. "Promise you won't be mad?" Jackson didn't say anything. She went on. "That teddy bear had a camera in it. I wanted to see if Emily was telling the truth. And I was right! So it was good I did it!" She touched his arm, but he jerked it away and turned to the TV again, clenching his jaw. She couldn't even trust him for one night. Not one night. How could they be best friends if she didn't trust him?

He was quiet for several moments before Jinx said in a scared voice, "Jackson?"

Slowly, he got up, his heart sinking into his feet. "Jinx, I asked you to trust me and you couldn't. What am I supposed to do with that? How can you call me your friend?"

Jinx's eyes got bright, a prelude to tears, he knew. Not that she would cry in front of him. She swallowed hard. "I do trust you, Jackson, just not other people. . . . In fact, you're the only one I trust."

Jackson looked away and then back down at Jinx. He knew he was the only one Jinx trusted, but even that had its limits. He wasn't doing Jinx any favors by coddling her—she had to get to know other people. She had to trust them. And she had to trust him *completely* if they were going to be best friends. "You betrayed me, Jinx. I asked you for one thing, and you couldn't even do that. I think we need to take some time apart."

Before Jinx could say anything, Jackson walked up the stairs. Before getting all the way up, he glanced back at Jinx and saw her staring off into space, a hopeless look on her face.

His heart broke into pieces, but his feet kept moving.

CHAPTER 20

Jinx ran up to her room, an empty feeling expanding in her gut. Time apart? Jackson wanted time apart? Was he breaking up their friendship? They'd been close for as long as Jinx could remember. She'd never known a time when he wasn't there. Jinx felt as if her eyeballs would come out. Tears streamed down her face as she slammed the door and threw herself on the bed.

It was so unfair! She'd uncovered the ruse, found out the truth, and here she was being punished.

The slow burn of anger started to replace the despair she felt. She welcomed the feeling. Being angry was way better than being sad. Anger got things done.

She wiped at her eyes and sat up on the bed. Fine. If he didn't want to be in her life, she wouldn't be in his. See how he liked it. A small voice in her head told her that she was in the wrong, but she ignored it. Wrong or right, they'd had their first paid investigation and found out, yet again, that everything was fake. She needed to blog this one—she had an obligation to her readers.

Going to her computer, she accessed the video feed from the teddy bear, the EVP recordings and EMF recordings. Then she opened a new file where she would document everything. She hadn't even looked at the EVP or the EMF after she'd watched the teddy video camera. What would have been the point?

As soon as Jinx began writing, she started feeling better. At least she was *doing* something—anger *did* get things done. She went through every second of the first night, making sure to note what the equipment found. About halfway through, right before Jinx knew the door would slam and Emily's hoax would begin, Jinx came across something . . . curious.

And then she remembered the time both she and Jackson felt the air change. The EMF reader went off the charts. The temperature dropped. How did Emily fake that? She also remembered the TV going on by itself. Looking at the EMF and EVP sensors again, she saw something there.

Quickly, she dialed Emily's number. On the third ring, Emily answered with a confused, "Hello?"

Jinx had no time for pleasantries. "Emily, does your TV go on and off by itself sometimes?"

Emily laughed a little bit. "Yeah, but Dad says it's because the place is so old. The wiring is just a little faulty."

Jinx sat back and didn't say anything for so long that Emily said "Hello?" again. Finally,

Jinx spoke up: "Emily, I think your place really is haunted."

Emily laughed again. "Nooo . . . Travis was haunting the place, remember? And anyway, we might be moving. Dad got a job offer in California over the weekend, during his trip. I'd be going with him. I'm so over this city. The only person I'll miss is Travis, but we're going to try to make it work."

Jinx waved that away. "As long as you get out of there."

"You really are into this stuff, huh?" Emily said. "I'll be fine. Also . . . thanks, Jinx. You're not as bad as you seem. I know I won't forget you."

Jinx smiled. Mission accomplished.

After she hung up, Jinx thought maybe she'd overreacted. Maybe some sort of wiring thing *did* happen. And maybe that caused an electromagnetic field to show up. Right when the TV went on. That would make sense.

To double-check, she decided to tweak her EVP software to see if she could hear anything through the TV static. She fast-forwarded it to the time when the TV turned on and the static played. She listened all the way through. About two minutes in, right when Jackson said "The clock stopped at 1:15," Jinx saw a little bleep.

Minimizing the levels on Jackson's voice, Jinx played the segment again.

A voice said, "You're next."

The hair on Jinx's neck stood straight up. That was not Travis's voice.

In fact, the voice didn't sound human at all. Emily's place was really haunted.

Ghosts were real.

Jinx sat back in her chair. Jackson may want some space, she thought, but there's no way he wouldn't want to hear about this.

She picked up her phone and dialed his number.

SEEK THE TRUTH
AND FIND THE CAUSE
WITH

THE PARANORMALISTS

CASE 1:
THE HAUNTING OF APARTMENT 101

Jinx was a social reject who became a punked-out paranormal investigator. Jackson is a jock by day and Jinx's ghost-hunting partner by night. When a popular girl named Emily asks the duo to explore a haunting in her dad's apartment, Jinx is skeptical—but Jackson insists they take the case. And the truth they find is even stranger than Emily's story.

CASE 2:
THE TERROR OF BLACK EAGLE TAVERN

Jinx's ghost-hunting partner Jackson may be a jock, but Jinx is not interested in helping his football buddy Todd—until Todd's case gets too weird to ignore. A supernatural presence is causing chaos at the bar Todd's family owns. And the threat has a connection to Todd that's deeper than even he realizes . . .

CASE 3:
THE MAYHEM ON MOHAWK AVENUE

Jinx and Jackson have become the go-to ghost hunters at their high school. When a new kid in town tries to get in on their business, Jinx is furious. Portland only needs one team to track down ghosties! But Jinx's quest to shut down her competition will lead her and Jackson down a dangerous path . . .

CASE 4:
THE BRIDGE OF DEATH

Jinx is the top paranormal investigator at her high school, and she has a blog to prove it. Jackson's her ghost-hunting partner by night—former partner, anyway. After a shakeup in the Paranormalists' operation, the two ex-best friends are on the outs, and at the worst possible time. Because a deadly supernatural threat is putting their classmates in harm's way . . .

AFTER THE DUST SETTLED

AFTER THE DUST SETTLED

PLAGUE RIDERS

AFTER THE DUST SETTLED

FIGHT THE WIND

AFTER THE DUST SETTLED

RIVER RUN

AFTER THE DUST SETTLED

PIG CITY

AFTER THE DUST SETTLED

SHOT DOWN

AFTER THE DUST SETTLED

SNAKEBITE

The world is over.
Can you survive what's next?

MEGAN ATWOOD

lives in Minneapolis, MN, and gets to write books for a living. She also teaches writing classes and reads as many young adult books as she can get her hands on. She only occasionally investigates paranormal activity.